Young People's Stories of Sharing

Sharing is... offering something of yours to someone else.

Sharing is... thinking about someone besides yourself.

Sharing is... listening while other people talk about their problems.

Sharing is... offering to help without thinking about a reward.

Sharing is... valued by people around the world.

Compiled by
Henry and Melissa Billings

Young People's Press
San Diego

Editorial, design and production by
Book Production Systems, Inc.

Cover illustration by Gwen Connelly.

Published in the United States of America.

3 4 5 6 7 8 9 – 99 98 97

ISBN 1-885658-22-2

Young People's
Stories of Sharing

This story comes from England. It shows that life is only beautiful when it is shared with others.

The Selfish Giant

Every afternoon children played in the Giant's garden. In it were soft green grass and beautiful flowers. There were twelve peach trees. Birds sat on the trees and sang sweetly. The children sometimes stopped their games in order to listen to the songs. "How happy we are here!" they cried to each other.

One day the Giant came back. He had been gone for seven years. When he arrived home, he saw the children playing in the garden.

"What are you doing there?" he cried in a very gruff voice. The children ran away.

"My own garden is my own garden," said the Giant. "Anyone can understand that. I will allow nobody to play in it but myself."

So he built a high wall all around the garden. He put up a sign that said, "STAY OUT."

He was a very selfish Giant.

Now the poor children had nowhere to play. They tried to play on the road. But the road was very dusty and full of hard stones. So they stood outside the garden wall and talked about the beautiful garden inside. "How happy we were there," they said to each other.

When Spring came, there were birds and blossoms all over the land. But in the garden of the selfish Giant it was still winter. The birds did not care to sing in it because there were no children. The trees forgot to blossom. Once a beautiful flower put its head out from the grass. But when it saw the sign it felt so sorry for the children that it slipped back into the ground again, and went off to sleep. The only people who were pleased were the Snow and the Frost.

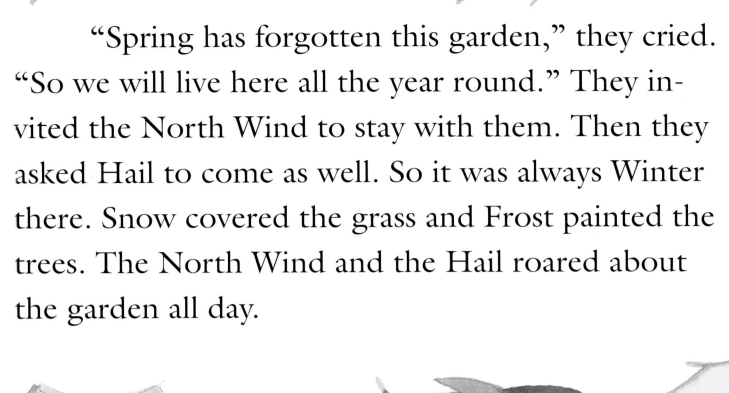

"Spring has forgotten this garden," they cried. "So we will live here all the year round." They invited the North Wind to stay with them. Then they asked Hail to come as well. So it was always Winter there. Snow covered the grass and Frost painted the trees. The North Wind and the Hail roared about the garden all day.

"I cannot understand why the Spring is so late in coming," said the Selfish Giant. He looked out at his cold white garden. "I hope there will be a change in the weather."

But the Spring never came.

One morning the Giant was lying in bed when he heard some lovely music. A songbird was singing outside his window. It had been a long time since the Giant had heard a bird sing in his garden. The song seemed to him to be the most beautiful music in the world.

"I believe the Spring has come at last," said the Giant. He jumped out of bed and looked out.

What did he see?

He saw a most wonderful sight. The children had crept into the garden through a little hole in the wall. They were sitting in the branches of the trees. And the trees were so glad to have the children back again that they had covered themselves with blossoms. The birds were flying about. The flowers were looking up through the green grass and laughing. It was a lovely scene. Only in one corner was it still winter. In that corner stood a little boy. He was so small that he could not reach up to the branches of the tree. He was wandering all around it, crying bitterly. The poor tree was still covered with frost and snow, and the North Wind was blowing and roaring about it.

"Climb up, little boy!" said the tree. It bent its branches down as low as it could. But the boy was too tiny to reach them.

And the Giant's heart melted as he looked out. "How selfish I have been!" he said. "Now I know why the Spring would not come here. I will put that poor little boy on the top of the tree. Then I will knock down the wall. And my garden shall be the children's playground forever and ever."

The Giant went quietly out into the garden. But when the children saw him they were frightened. They all ran away. The garden became winter again. Only the little boy did not run, for his eyes were so full of tears that he did not see the Giant coming.

The Giant crept up behind him. He took him gently in his hand and put him up into the tree. The tree broke at once into blossom. Birds came and sang on it. The little boy stretched out his two arms and flung them around the Giant's neck. He kissed the Giant.

The other children saw that the Giant was not wicked any longer. They came running back. With them came the Spring.

"It is your garden now, little children," said the Giant. He took a great axe and knocked down the wall. And when people went to market that day they found the Giant playing with the children in the most beautiful garden they had ever seen.

At the beginning of the story, the Giant is quite selfish. He refuses to let the children play in his garden. He wants to enjoy his garden all by himself. But what he gets is constant cold, wind, and snow. None of the trees, flowers, or birds want to share their beauty with such a selfish person. The Giant learns from his mistake. He sees that only by sharing will his life be filled with beauty. It isn't easy for the Giant to share. When he tries, he finds that the children are afraid of him. But the Giant proves he has changed. He helps the little boy into the tree. For sharing with the children, the Giant is rewarded with the most beautiful garden ever.

How Sun, Moon, and Wind Went Out to Dinner

This story comes from India. In it, selfish children are punished and a sharing child is rewarded.

One day Sun, Moon, and Wind went out to eat with their uncle and aunt, Thunder and Lightning. Their mother, Star, waited at home for them to return.

Now both Sun and Wind were selfish. They thought only about themselves. They enjoyed the great meal that had been fixed for them. They did not think about saving even a crumb to take home to their mother.

Gentle Moon, however, did not forget Star. Moon wished to share the wonderful meal with her mother. So each time a dish was brought to Moon, she placed a little bit of it under one of her beautiful long fingernails.

When the children returned home, Star said, "Well, children, what have you brought home for me?"

Then Sun said, "I have brought nothing home for you. I went out to enjoy myself with my friends—not to bring home a dinner for my mother!"

And Wind said, "I have not brought anything, either. You could hardly expect me to think of you—I was busy with my own pleasure."

But Moon said, "Mother, fetch a plate. I will show you what I have brought you." And shaking her hands, she showered down the most delicious dinner ever seen.

Then Star turned to Sun and spoke firmly.
"Because you went out to enjoy yourself, without any
thought of your mother at home, you shall be cursed.
From now on, your rays shall be hot and scorching, and
shall burn all that they touch. People shall hate you.
They shall cover their heads when you appear."

(And that is why the Sun is so hot to this day.)

Then Star turned to Wind and said, "You also forgot your mother in the middle of your selfish pleasures. You also shall be cursed. You shall always blow in the hot dry weather, and shall dry up all living things. People shall hate you. They shall avoid you forever."

(And that is why the Wind in the hot weather is still so unpleasant.)

At last Star turned to Moon. "Daughter, you remembered your mother. You kept a share for me even as you enjoyed your own meal. From now on, you shall be ever cool, and calm, and bright. No hard glare shall come from your pure rays. People shall always call you 'blessed.' "

(And that is why the Moon's light is so soft, and cool, and beautiful even to this day.)

This story shows that sharing is always important. Sharing is not something you do only when you feel like it or only when it is convenient. As a family member, you should always be willing to share. Moon went out of her way to save some food for her mother. She remembered her mother even during an evening that was set up for her own enjoyment.

THE IMPORTANCE OF SHARING

This story comes from the Nkundo people of Zaire. It tells about the importance of sharing within your family.

One day Wanga and Balenge went into the forest to gather plants. Young Bokune went with them. She could learn many things from her two older sisters.

As they went, going, going, down the path, Balenge and Wanga saw a snake. It was an *ndota* snake. Its meat would make a delicious meal. Quickly they killed it. Then Balenge and Wanga said, "Let's not take it home to Father. We would have to share it with the whole family. Father would get the best part. We would not get much at all."

So the two girls cooked the snake. But they refused to give any of it to Bokune.

Bokune asked, "Why won't you share your meat with me?"

"You did not work for it," they said.

The three girls went on into the forest. They filled their baskets with plants, then headed home. Said Balenge, "When we get home, we won't tell anyone that we killed a snake."

Wanga agreed. "It was very good meat, and they won't like it if they know we had it."

When they reached a village, everyone greeted them. "All of you, Balenge, Wanga, Bokune, you have all come."

"Yes. We have come."

Bokune began to sing,

> We saw a really good snake.
> They didn't hear me.
> We killed the snake.
> They refused me.
> They didn't hear me.

Soon the girls came to another village. Again people came out to meet them.

Bokune again began to sing her song. Balenge and Wanga said, "Stop! It is bad when you talk about the *ndota*."

The girls went and went and went, *te-e-e*, until they came to the house of their father. They sat to talk with him a little. He said, "Balenge and Wanga, you had a good journey with Bokune?"

Before they could answer, Bokune began her song again.

Their father asked, "What about this song of Bokune?"

"It doesn't mean anything," said Balenge and Wanga.

But Bokune said, "They killed a snake. It was an *ndota*, Father, the kind you like best. They cut it up and cooked it, but they gave none to me."

Their father was very upset. "You are very bad children," he said to Balenge and Wanga. "You killed a good snake, the kind we like best. You ate it. You did not bring it home to us."

The father truly felt that they were bad.

Any child that eats in secret and does not share is not worthy of the family.

As this story reminds us, happy families are based on sharing. Mothers and fathers share their love, their home, their food, and many other things with their children. Children also must share with their parents and among themselves. When Balenge and Wanga killed the snake, they should have brought it home so the whole family could share it.

Acknowledgments

Grateful acknowledgment is made for permission to reprint the following copyrighted material:

"The Importance of Sharing," adapted for readability from *"On Another Day . . . ": Tales Told Among the Nkundo of Zaire,* by Mabel H. Ross and Barbara K. Walker. (Hamden, CT: The Shoe String Press [an Archon Book], 1979), © Mabel H. Ross and Barbara K. Walker, used by permission of the authors, now holders of all rights.